Love Stinks!

by Nancy Krulik • illustrated by John & Wendy

For *my* valentine, from your
not-so-secret admirer—N.K.

For Karen, a real sweetheart!—J&W

Text copyright © 2004 by Nancy Krulik. Illustrations copyright © 2004 by
John and Wendy. All rights reserved. Published by Grosset & Dunlap, a
division of Penguin Young Readers Group, 345 Hudson Street, New York,
New York 10014. GROSSET & DUNLAP is a trademark of Penguin Group
(USA) Inc. Printed in the U.S.A.

Library of Congress Cataloging-in-Publication Data

Krulik, Nancy E.

Love stinks! / by Nancy Krulik ; illustrated by John & Wendy.

p. cm. — (Katie Kazoo, switcheroo ; 15)
Summary: When the magic wind turns fourth-grader Katie, who dislikes
the "mushy gushy stuff" of Valentine's Day, into a candy store owner, she
decides to write her own "love messages" on the candy hearts.
ISBN 0-448-43640-X (pbk.)
[1. Valentine's Day—Fiction. 2. Magic—Fiction. 3. Candy—Fiction.]
I. John & Wendy. II. Title. III. Series.

PZ7.K9416Lo 2004
[Fic]—dc22   2004015226

ISBN 0-448-43640-X   10 9

Chapter 1

"So are you playing goalie at your soccer game today?" Katie Carew asked her best friend Jeremy Fox. They were walking home from school together after band practice on Monday afternoon.

Jeremy didn't answer Katie. Instead he dropped his head and ducked behind her. "Hide me!" he whispered.

"From what?" Katie asked him.

"From *Becky*. She's coming this way."

Everyone in the fourth grade knew that Becky Stern had a crush on Jeremy. Jeremy didn't like Becky at all. But this was the first time he'd ever actually hidden from her.

Katie giggled. "Oh, come on. She's not that bad."

"You want to bet?" Jeremy said. "She's been following me for two weeks! She keeps talking to me about Valentine's Day." He ducked down even farther.

Now Katie understood. Valentine's Day was this Saturday. Becky was probably hoping that Jeremy would be her valentine. Considering Jeremy was *hiding* from Becky, Katie doubted that would ever happen.

Unfortunately, Becky spotted Jeremy behind Katie. "There you are," she called out to him in her soft Southern accent. "I've been looking all over for you."

"Why?" Jeremy asked her.

"To give you these." Becky held out a clear plastic bag filled with chocolate kisses. "I saw them at Cinnamon's Candy Shop and thought of you."

Jeremy frowned. "No, thanks. I don't eat candy. I'm in training."

Katie tried hard not to laugh. That hadn't stopped him before. Just yesterday he'd eaten a whole bag of gumdrops!

But Becky wasn't insulted that Jeremy wouldn't take her gift. In fact, she seemed impressed. "Oh, Jeremy, you've got such willpower," she cooed. "I should be in training for my gymnastics classes, too. We're working on backflips. Look what I learned this week." Becky turned around to make sure no one was coming and flipped in the air, right in the middle of the sidewalk!

"That was really good!" Katie said.

Becky smiled. "Thanks. What did *you* think, Jeremy?"

"It was okay," Jeremy mumbled. His face was redder than Katie's hair! "I . . . um . . . I gotta get going. I've got a soccer game."

"Oh, okay," Becky said. "Well, see ya later . . . Happy almost Valentine's Day!"

Jeremy rolled his eyes and walked off. Katie hurried to catch up to him.

"You see what I mean?" Jeremy asked her.

"I'd say she definitely *flipped* for you!" Katie joked.

Jeremy groaned.

"Don't worry. Valentine's Day will be over soon," Katie told him. "She won't bug you so much after that."

"I hope not," Jeremy said.

"I can't believe you gave up a whole bag of chocolate kisses. They looked delicious."

"It wasn't hard," Jeremy assured her. "I'm still full from yesterday. Can you believe how much candy we ate?"

"I didn't eat that much."

"Only three licorice sticks, a bunch of sour lemon drops, and a rainbow-colored lollipop," Jeremy reminded her.

"Oh, yeah. I forgot about the lollipop," Katie said. She licked her lips. "Cinnamon's Candy Shop has the best lollipops."

Jeremy nodded. "I'm so glad Cinnamon decided to open a candy store in the mall."

Katie knew exactly what he meant. Cinnamon's Candy Shop was located right across from the Book Nook, the store Katie's mom managed. It was a fun place to hang out while Katie waited for her mom to finish with work. Sometimes Katie brought her friends, like Jeremy and Suzanne Lock, to hang out there with her.

Cinnamon was really nice. She let Katie dip strawberries into dark chocolate or fill the penny candy drawers with bubble gum, hard candies, and tiny chocolate bars. Best of all, she always gave Katie free lemon drops.

"You'd better hope Becky doesn't visit Cinnamon's Candy Shop this week," Katie told Jeremy.

"Why not?"

"Cinnamon is selling giant candy hearts," she explained. "She'll put any message you want right on the heart. Cinnamon guarantees to have the heart delivered in time for Valentine's Day!"

"That would be so embarrassing!" Jeremy exclaimed.

"Well, if Becky does send you a heart, at

least it will be delicious." Katie was trying to make him feel better.

But it didn't work. "I hate Valentine's Day!" Jeremy grumbled.

Chapter 2

But not all the fourth-graders hated Valentine's Day. In fact, Wednesday afternoon, right after her cooking class, Katie hurried over to Suzanne's house. She, Becky, Emma Weber, and Jessica Haynes were all getting together with Suzanne to make valentines for their friends.

"Oh, that's a cute one," Emma said as she looked at the long, thin, squiggly-shaped card Katie was working on. "It looks just like Slinky."

Suzanne looked curiously at Katie. "You made a valentine for a *snake*?"

"Of course," Katie told her. "Animals need

love, too. I even made one for my dog, Pepper."

"Pepper's cute, but Slinky is creepy," Suzanne said with a shudder.

"Slinky is *not* creepy!" Katie insisted.

"I'm glad *our* class has a guinea pig. I love Fuzzy," Suzanne boasted.

Suzanne was always bragging about what was happening in class 4B. But Katie didn't care. She was glad Suzanne was happy in her classroom. Katie was certainly happy in hers.

Class 4A was a very different kind of classroom. Katie had never been in one like it before. Her teacher, Mr. Guthrie, wasn't very strict. He let the kids sit in beanbag chairs instead of at desks. He thought they learned better when they were comfortable.

Mr. Guthrie did other cool stuff, like letting George Brennan and Kadeem Carter have joke-telling contests. He called them joke-offs. And Mr. Guthrie had gotten the class the coolest pet in the whole school—Slinky the snake. The kids had raised him ever since he'd hatched from his egg.

"Look what I made for Jeremy," Becky announced, interrupting Katie's thoughts. She leaped to her feet and held up a giant red construction paper heart with lace trim. "Do you think he'll like it?"

Katie knew Jeremy would hate getting a huge card from Becky. But she didn't tell her that. Katie didn't like to hurt people's feelings.

"I don't know what you see in Jeremy," Suzanne said. "He's such a jerk."

"That's mean, Suzanne," Katie told her.

Suzanne shrugged. "He's *your* best friend, Katie. Not mine."

Katie nodded. That was the truth. Suzanne and Jeremy were both Katie's best friends. But they didn't always like each other very much.

"Who are you making valentines for, Suzanne?" Jessica asked her.

"Just for my very best friends," she said. "I don't want to waste time making cards for people who aren't going to give *me* one."

"That makes sense," Jessica said. "Oh, and just so you know, I'm making one for you."

Emma W. was busy making her valentines. "Do you have any more pink construction paper?" she asked.

"Sure," Suzanne told her. "It's over there,

next to Heather's play kitchen." She pointed to a little plastic kitchen that was filled with plastic food, pots, and pans.

Heather was Suzanne's one-year-old sister. Lately, Suzanne's whole house had begun to look like a toy store. There were stuffed animals, rag dolls, and big rubber balls all over the place.

Emma certainly didn't mind. She had three younger brothers. She knew what it was like to live with a lot of toys around. She just stepped over the dolls and balls to reach the construction paper. "My twin brothers have the same kitchen," she told Suzanne. "But theirs isn't as nice. It's a hand-me-down."

"That one's brand-new," Suzanne told her. "My parents are always buying new toys for Heather." She sounded a little jealous.

Ding dong. Just then, the doorbell rang.

"I'll get it," Suzanne called out, loud enough for her mother to hear. She leaped up from the table and raced for the door.

When Suzanne returned, she was carrying a big cardboard box in her hand.

"It's a package from Cinnamon's Candy Shop," Suzanne announced. "And it's addressed to me!"

"Oh, yummy," Becky said. "Who sent it?"

"I don't know," Suzanne replied as she looked at the box.

"Is there a card or anything?" Emma W. asked.

"Maybe it's on the inside," Jessica suggested. "Open it."

"Okay, okay, don't rush me!" Suzanne exclaimed excitedly. She carefully began to open the box. "It's one of those giant candy hearts!"

Katie looked down at the sugary pink heart. It looked just like the little pink candy message hearts Cinnamon sold at the store. But this heart was the size of a small cake!

Cinnamon had etched a picture of a bumble bee and the word MINE onto the heart. "Be mine," Katie realized.

"A candy valentine!" Jessica squealed. "Who is it from?"

Suzanne picked up a small white envelope from the bottom of the box. "It says, 'Happy Valentine's Day from your secret admirer.' "

"Wow!" Becky exclaimed. "A secret admirer. I wish I had one of those."

Suzanne laughed. "Come on, Becky. It's no secret who *you'd* like to get candy from."

Becky blushed while all the girls giggled.

All except Katie, that is. She was getting really tired of hearing about how much Becky liked Jeremy. After all, Jeremy was her best friend. And Becky was making him really unhappy.

"So who do you think the admirer is?" Emma asked Suzanne.

"Maybe it's a boy in our class," Jessica suggested.

"It could be an older boy. Like in the *fifth* grade," Emma W. thought out loud.

"I don't know," Suzanne said. "It's a mystery."

"We'll figure out who it is," Jessica assured Suzanne. "Starting tomorrow, we're all going to look around and see if any of the boys are paying special attention to you."

"Maybe he doesn't go to our school," Suzanne quickly suggested.

"Then where would he be from?" Becky asked.

Suzanne said with a shrug, "He could be from anywhere."

Katie rolled her eyes and looked over at her best friend. Suzanne was clearly enjoying all the attention. But she didn't seem as excited by the candy heart as Katie thought she might be.

There was something weird about this whole secret admirer thing. Katie just couldn't figure out what it was.

Chapter 3

First thing Thursday morning, Katie and most of the girls in the fourth grade gathered on the playground. But Katie wasn't happy. All anyone could talk about was Suzanne's secret admirer. Emma, Becky, and Jessica must have been on the phone all night telling people about it. Katie really didn't care about Suzanne's secret admirer.

When Kevin Camilleri walked by, Jessica turned her attention to him.

"Hey, Kevin," Jessica called out. "What do you think of Suzanne?" she asked.

Kevin frowned. "I think she's a snob."

"So you're not her secret admirer?"

"If I am, it's a secret to me!" Kevin ran off to kick a soccer ball with Andrew Epstein.

"We can cross Kevin off our list," Jessica said.

Emma W. nodded. "You can cross George Brennan off, too. I called him last night. He doesn't like Suzanne very much."

"Do you think it could be Jeremy?" Jessica asked Katie. "He's your best friend, so you should know."

Katie shook her head. "I don't think so."

"That's a relief," Becky said.

"I've already talked to Andrew and Kadeem," Emma W. told the girls. "They didn't even know Cinnamon was making big candy hearts. So neither of them could be the secret admirer."

Katie sighed. She really didn't want to talk about this anymore. Katie was tired of hearing about all the mushy, lovey-dovey stuff. She was already sick of Valentine's Day . . . and it hadn't even come yet!

At just that moment, Suzanne strolled onto the playground. She was holding a small white envelope in her hand.

"Hi, everyone," she greeted the crowd of girls.

"Hi, Suzanne," Jessica replied. "We've been talking to all the boys in the fourth grade. So far, we haven't been able to figure out who your secret admirer is."

"Well, maybe this will help," she said, holding out the white envelope. "I found it in my mailbox this morning."

Katie wondered why Suzanne had been looking in her mailbox first thing in the morning. The mail usually didn't get delivered until after they were in school.

Jessica took the envelope from Suzanne. Inside was a note made up of letters that were cut from magazines. It read:

Be Mine.

From,
Your Secret Admirer

"Wow!" Miriam exclaimed.

"That's so romantic," Becky added.

"Well, I guess we won't be able to figure out who he is from his handwriting," Katie said.

"He's good at keeping his identity a secret," Emma W. noted. "I'll bet he's really smart."

"Well, that leaves out any of the fourth-grade boys," Jessica joked. "None of them are very smart."

Just then, the school bell rang. "We're not going to be able to solve this now," Suzanne told the others. "It's time to go inside."

Becky turned just as Jeremy, Kevin, and Manny Gonzalez were walking by.

"Hey, Jeremy," she called.

"Hi, Becky," Jeremy mumbled back.

"Are you going to our cooking club meeting Saturday?" she asked. Every Saturday some of the kids in the fourth grade met at Katie's house to cook. Sometimes they used recipes from Katie's Wednesday after-school cooking class or sometimes they just made their own creations. Either way, it was a lot of fun.

"I've got a soccer game in the morning," he told her. "But I'll probably come after."

"Oh, good, I'm going to the meeting, too. Maybe we can cook a Valentine's Day treat together," Becky said hopefully.

Jeremy blushed.

Katie sighed. It was obvious Becky had made Jeremy uncomfortable . . . again!

But Becky didn't seem to notice. "See you in class," she told him. Then she ran off into the school building with Suzanne and Jessica.

"Oh, Jeremy, that sounds soooo romantic," George teased.

"Yeah," Manny added. He batted his eyelashes wildly. "We can cook together. *Oooo.*"

Katie watched Jeremy's face. She could tell he didn't think George and Manny were very funny.

"I wish there was no such thing as Valentine's Day!" he shouted out angrily.

Katie gasped. Jeremy had just made a wish. That could mean real trouble!

Katie knew that sometimes wishes came true. And not the way you meant them to, either.

Katie's troubles with wishes all started

one day at the beginning of third grade. Katie had lost the football game for her team, ruined her favorite pair of pants, and let out a big burp in front of the whole class. That night, Katie had wished she could be anyone but herself.

There must have been a shooting star overhead when she made that wish, because the very next day the magic wind came.

The magic wind was a wild tornado that blew just around Katie. It was so powerful that every time it came, it turned her into somebody else! Katie never knew when the wind would arrive. But when it did, her whole world was turned upside down . . . *switcheroo*!

The first time the magic wind came, it turned Katie into Speedy, the hamster in her third-grade class! Katie escaped from the hamster cage and wound up in the boys' locker room! Good thing the magic wind turned Katie back into herself before the boys found out a girl had been in there!

The magic wind came back again and again after that. Sometimes it changed Katie into other kids—like Jeremy, Emma W., Becky, and Suzanne. Other times it turned her into adults—like Lucille the lunch lady, Principal Kane, and the school music teacher, Mr. Starkey. That had been an *especially* bad time. The kids in the band definitely did not make beautiful music while Katie was conducting.

That was why Katie didn't make wishes anymore. She didn't want them to come true.

Luckily, Jeremy's wish *hadn't* come true. All of the kids' beanbag chairs were covered with hearts, cupids, and other Valentine's Day decorations.

There would be a Valentine's Day. At least in class 4A.

Chapter 4

"Can I come to the mall with you today after school?" Suzanne asked Katie as the girls left school together at the end of the day. Suzanne knew that Katie often hung out at the mall on Thursdays. That was the day Mrs. Carew worked late at the Book Nook.

"Sure. My mom's picking me up in a few minutes," Katie told her. "Don't you have to ask permission?"

Suzanne nodded. She pulled a small silver phone from her backpack. "My mom said I could borrow her phone today," Suzanne told her. "Just in case I wanted to go home with someone after school."

"I thought cell phones weren't allowed in school," Katie reminded her.

"I kept it hidden in my backpack," Suzanne replied. "No one even knew it was there."

"Hey, what are you guys doing?" Jessica asked as she, Mandy, and Becky walked over.

Suzanne put her finger to her lips. "*Shhh.* I can't hear."

"She's calling her mom to see if she can go to the mall with me," Katie whispered.

"Cool," Jessica said. "Can I come, too?"

Katie nodded. "If your mom says it's okay."

"How about me?" Becky asked.

Katie shrugged. "Sure. And you, too, if you want, Mandy."

"Oh, this will be great!" Becky exclaimed. "When we get to the mall, we can talk to Cinnamon about Suzanne's secret admirer. Since Cinnamon made the heart, she's *got* to know who he is!"

"Do we have to keep talking about Valentine's Day?" Katie asked them.

"What else is there to talk about?" Becky asked her.

Katie sighed. The girls were really making her crazy. She wished she could spend the day with Jeremy. She was sure he wouldn't bring up Valentine's Day once.

As the girls borrowed Suzanne's cell phone to call home, Katie spotted Jeremy, George, Kevin, and Manny walking in the distance. She ran over to them.

"Hey, guys," she said. She turned to Jeremy. "I'm going to the mall. Cinnamon said I could help her put the new lollipops into the display case. Do you want to help?"

Jeremy looked over to where the girls were all gathered around Suzanne and her cell phone.

"Not if *they're* going," he told her, pointing to the girls.

"Why not?"

Before Jeremy could answer, George puckered up his lips really tight. "Oh, Jeremy,

I love you!" he said in a fake Southern accent.

"You're such a *lover boy*," Kevin added.

"Lover boy, I love you," Manny joked.

"That's why I'm not going to the mall," Jeremy groaned. "Cut it out!" he warned the boys.

"We were just joking," George told him.

"It wasn't funny," Jeremy told him. Then he turned to Katie. "I'm not going anywhere near Becky."

"Why don't you go off with the other girls, Katie Kazoo," George said, using the nickname he'd given her. "You can try and figure out who Suzanne's secret admirer is."

"Whoever he is, he's pretty dumb," Kevin said. "Who would want Suzanne for a valentine?"

"Maybe it's Jeremy," Manny suggested. "He's the fourth-grade lover boy." He kissed the air again.

Now Jeremy was really angry. He rolled his hand up into a fist and stared angrily at Manny. "I dare you to say that again," he warned, staring Manny straight in the face.

Katie was surprised. She'd never seen

Jeremy this angry. "Gosh, I'm sorry," Manny said, quickly stepping back.

"You'd better be," Jeremy said, walking away. "I'm going home."

Katie watched as Jeremy stormed off by himself. Valentine's Day was supposed to be about love. Instead, it was making everyone hate one another.

Valentine's Day was a real pain!

Chapter 5

"Hi, girls," Cinnamon greeted Katie, Suzanne, Becky, Mandy, and Jessica as they arrived at the candy store later that afternoon.

Katie sniffed at the air. "*Mmm*. It always smells so yummy in here."

"You must be hungry for some candy," Cinnamon teased.

Katie grinned. Cinnamon was just the kind of person who should own a candy store. Her short brown hair was tinted with just a little bit of spicy red, sort of like gingerbread. Her eyes were as blue as blue raspberry lollipops, and her lips were as red as Red Hots.

Most important of all, Cinnamon was a really sweet person.

"Forget the candy," Jessica interrupted. "We have something more important to talk to you about."

"More important than candy? Impossible," Cinnamon joked.

"Seriously," Becky told her. "This is *big*. We have a mystery to solve."

"Oh." Cinnamon sat down on a stool. "It *does* sound important."

"Suzanne has a secret admirer," Becky confided. "And you're the only person who may know who he is."

"Me?" Cinnamon asked. "How would I know?"

"Because he sent her one of your candy

hearts," Mandy explained.

Katie looked over at Suzanne. She was busy looking at the penny candy. She wasn't at all interested in the conversation the girls were having with Cinnamon. That seemed strange to Katie. She would have thought Suzanne would be dying to hear what Cinnamon had to say.

"Can you check your receipts and see who bought that heart?" Jessica asked Cinnamon, interrupting Katie's thoughts.

"I can't do that," Cinnamon told her.

The girls all looked at her, surprised.

Cinnamon shook her head. "I never tell secrets. Especially secrets about secret admirers."

Just then, Suzanne walked over to the group. "I just remembered I have to ask my mother something. I'm going to call her from outside the store. The reception is better out-side the shop. I'll be right back."

As Suzanne left the store, the girls all

began picking out penny candy. "Hey, Katie, can you do me a favor?" Cinnamon asked.

"Sure," Katie replied. "What do you need me to do?"

"Could you go over to Louie's and get me a slice of pizza?" she asked. "I'm starving." She handed Katie some dollar bills from her purse.

Katie was amazed that Cinnamon could be hungry with all the candy around! Still, Katie was always willing to do a favor for Cinnamon. "Sure," she said, taking the money. "I'll be back in a minute."

$\times$ $\times$ $\times$

Louie's Pizzeria was next to the Book Nook, just across the way from Cinnamon's Candy Shop. It took Katie only a minute to get there and buy a slice of pizza.

As she walked back toward the candy store, Katie spotted Suzanne. She was hunched down, hiding behind a tall plant. It was pretty obvious she didn't want anyone

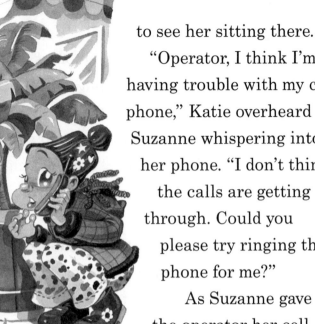

to see her sitting there.

"Operator, I think I'm having trouble with my cell phone," Katie overheard Suzanne whispering into her phone. "I don't think the calls are getting through. Could you please try ringing the phone for me?"

As Suzanne gave the operator her cell phone number, Katie quietly snuck into the candy shop and handed the slice of pizza to Cinnamon.

"Thanks, Katie," Cinnamon said. "You're the best."

A moment later, Suzanne walked back into the store.

"Did you get your mom?" Jessica asked her.

Before Suzanne could answer, her cell phone rang. "Hello?" she answered the phone. Then her eyes opened wide with surprise. "How did you get this number?"

"Oh my gosh, is it him?" Jessica squealed.

Suzanne nodded but put her finger to her lips to make Jessica be quiet.

"But how did you know I would have a cell phone with me today?" Suzanne asked. Then she giggled. "You are smart."

"Ask him what his name is," Becky suggested.

"What's your name?" Suzanne said into the phone. She listened for a minute. Then she said. "Oh, come on, tell me."

Katie turned away and frowned. Of course the person on the other end wasn't going to tell Suzanne his name. That's because there *wasn't* any person on the other line. It was just the operator testing the ring on Suzanne's cell phone.

Now Katie understood why this whole secret admirer thing had seemed so weird. Suzanne didn't have a secret admirer at all!

She'd made the whole thing up just to get attention. She'd probably even sent herself that candy heart! And the other girls had fallen for the whole thing!

"Suzanne, this is so exciting," Becky cooed as Suzanne hung up the phone. "You know what? I'm going to order a special candy heart for Jeremy. Can I do that now, Cinnamon?"

Cinnamon handed Becky a form. "Just fill this out," she told her. "I'll make sure it's delivered to your valentine by Saturday. Be sure to give me his address."

"Oh, I don't have his address," Becky said. "Can't you deliver it to school?"

"Hmm," said Cinnamon, looking at her watch. "I don't have much time, but if I hurry I can have it delivered to your school tomorrow," Cinnamon answered.

Katie gulped. She knew Jeremy would be really mad if a heart got delivered to him right in front of all his school friends. "No, don't," she warned Becky. But the girls just ignored her!

"I'm going to order a special candy heart, too," Jessica said, taking one of Cinnamon's forms.

"For who?" Suzanne and Becky asked together.

Jessica grinned. "I'm not telling. *I'm* going to be someone's secret admirer."

"That's a good idea," Mandy said. She took a piece of paper from the counter and began scribbling down *her* message. "I know just who to send one to."

"I didn't know you had a crush on anyone," Suzanne told Mandy.

"*Andrew* didn't know it, either. But he will now," Mandy laughed.

Suzanne, Becky, and Jessica all started to giggle.

But not Katie. "This is a bad idea," she warned. "None of the boys will like getting candy at school."

"You're just saying that because you don't have a crush on anyone," Jessica told her.

"And no boy likes her, either," Becky added.

"They do, too," Katie said.

"Sure they do, Katie," Suzanne assured her friend. "But the boys like you as a pal. Not like a *valentine*."

Katie wanted to shout out that no one liked Suzanne like a valentine, either. Her secret admirer was a big fake! But Katie couldn't do that. It would be too mean.

Instead, she turned and walked out of the store. "I'm going back to Louie's for a veggie slice," she told the other girls angrily.

As Katie stormed across the mall, she grew madder and madder. She was sick and tired of Valentine's Day. It was nothing but trouble!

That was it! Katie wasn't celebrating Valentine's Day. She wasn't going to eat any little candy hearts, wear red all day, or make any more cards! As far as Katie was concerned, there was no Valentine's Day. She was calling the whole thing off!

Chapter 6

"Hey there, Katie!" Louie exclaimed cheerfully as she walked into his restaurant. "Back again so soon? Cinnamon must be really hungry."

Katie tried to smile. But it was hard. "This time I'm getting a slice of pizza for myself. My mother gave me five dollars to spend while I'm at the mall." She sighed and plopped onto one of the stools at the counter.

"Bad day, huh?" Louie asked her.

"The worst," Katie agreed. "I hate Valentine's Day."

Louie nodded and ran his finger over his thick, dark mustache. "Ah. So you have a love problem. Do you have a crush on someone?"

Katie made a face. "Louie! I'm only in fourth grade. I'm too young to be in love."

"I agree," Louie said.

"I wish somebody would tell that to Suzanne, Becky, Mandy, and Jessica though," Katie sighed. "Love is all they talk about these days."

"And that's a bad thing?"

Katie nodded. "*Really* bad. Because of them, Jeremy won't hang out with me. He doesn't want to be near Becky. And some of the other boys are going to be really upset when they find out that they're getting candy hearts at school!"

"They're definitely not going to like that," Louie agreed.

"You wouldn't believe all the weird stuff Suzanne's been doing just because it's Valentine's Day," Katie continued.

"Oh, I don't know," Louie said. "I've seen Suzanne do some pretty odd things."

"Not like this," Katie assured him.

"Well, I know what will cheer you up," Louie told her. "I'll make you a super veggie special—with extra spinach."

Katie looked around. The restaurant was empty. "You're going to make a whole pie, just for me?" she asked him, surprised.

Louie nodded. "You're my favorite customer. You deserve it. Besides, I just had a huge crowd of college boys in here. They ate all the ready-made pies I had. I've got to make a few new ones. You can help me. I'll let you sprinkle on the cheese."

Katie smiled. Louie always made her feel better.

"Wait here. I'll go in the back and get some more mushrooms and veggies."

"Okay," Katie told him. She sat back in her seat and watched as Louie headed into the back room. She was glad to be alone for a minute. At least she wouldn't have to hear anyone talking about Valentine's Day.

Suddenly, Katie felt a light breeze blowing on the back of her neck. She pulled the collar of her jacket up. But that didn't stop the breeze from blowing on her. In fact, it seemed to get stronger.

Whoosh! Within seconds, the breeze was no longer light and airy. It was more like a powerful burst of wind. A tornado-like wind . . . that was only swirling around Katie.

Katie gulped. This wasn't just any wind. This was the magic wind!

The whirling tornado grew stronger and stronger, blowing around Katie so powerfully that she had to hold her hands over her face to keep her hair from being blown into her eyes. She tensed up her body and tried to keep from being blown away.

And then it stopped. Just like that.

The magic wind was gone.

And so was Katie Carew.

Chapter 7

Katie sat there for a minute, afraid to open her eyes. She sniffed at the air. *Mmm.* Something smelled good.

It wasn't a tangy pizza smell, though. It was sweeter and richer . . . like chocolate.

Slowly, Katie opened her eyes and looked around. She was surrounded by vats of warm melted chocolate, fresh strawberries, and boxes of candy. Katie was in the tiny kitchen in the back of Cinnamon's Candy Shop.

Okay, so that explained *where* she was. But it didn't explain *who* she was.

"Cinnamon," Katie heard Suzanne's voice coming from the front of the store.

"Cinnamon, where are you?" Suzanne called again. Her voice got louder as she came into the kitchen. "Oh, there you are."

Katie looked around. Cinnamon wasn't in the back room.

Or was she? As Katie looked down, she could see she was wearing Cinnamon's cheery red-and-white checkered apron over a pair of cherry red pants. The green nail polish Katie had been wearing was gone. Instead, her fingernails were coated with traces of chocolate.

Katie had turned into Cinnamon!

"Are you okay?" Suzanne asked her.

Katie gulped. She was definitely *not* okay. She didn't want to be Cinnamon. Not right now. Not when she was supposed to be making Valentine's Day candies!

"Cinnamon?" Suzanne repeated.

"Yes?" Katie answered finally.

Suzanne handed Katie three sheets of paper and fifteen dollars. "Here are their order forms and the money from Jessica, Mandy, and Becky. We're going to go now. My mom's picking us up."

Katie was surprised. "I thought you were going home with my . . . I mean *Katie's* mom," she told Suzanne. *Whoops. That was close.*

"Her mom doesn't leave work until seven o'clock, and Becky, Jessica, and Mandy don't have any money left to spend. If they can't shop, we may as well leave," Suzanne explained. "Besides, we're going back to my house to talk about our crushes. Katie wouldn't want to do that."

That made Katie mad. Suzanne was her best friend. And she was leaving her out of everything!

"Yeah, well, I'm glad you're going," Katie said angrily.

"What?" Suzanne asked.

Oops. Katie gulped. The real Cinnamon never would have gotten mad at Suzanne. "I mean, as soon as you leave, I can make those hearts. I've got to hurry. The mail carrier will be here soon."

✕ ✕ ✕

The minute the girls left the candy shop, Katie locked the door and turned the sign on the door so it read CLOSED. She didn't want to have to pretend to be Cinnamon for all the store's customers.

Then she plopped down on the floor near the penny candy bins and frowned. Everything had gone wrong today. And to top it all off, the magic wind had come and turned her into Cinnamon!

Hmmm. Katie thought about that for a minute. Actually, being Cinnamon wasn't all bad. At least she could eat as much candy as she wanted. After all, she owned the store.

Katie walked over to the lemon-drop bin, and took a big handful. Next, she decided to munch on jelly beans. *Mmm* . . . the red ones tasted like strawberries. Katie took *two* handfuls of those.

After the jelly beans, Katie popped two Red Hots in her mouth at the same time. YIKES! Those were hotter than she'd thought they would be. Just then, Katie spotted some heart-shaped, chocolate-covered mints on the counter. A cool mint was the perfect thing to soothe a hot mouth. Katie took a handful of those, too . . .

Oooh. Suddenly, Katie didn't feel so good. Her stomach hurt. And she had a headache. It figured. Those stupid *heart-shaped* candies had gotten her sick! Even further proof that there should be no Valentine's Day!

Angrily, Katie grabbed the candy order forms her friends had filled out. "LOVE STINKS!" she shouted as she tore them into little pieces.

Chapter 8

Katie sat there for a moment, staring at the pile of shredded paper she had just made. She couldn't believe what she'd done! Why did she rip up the forms? She was Cinnamon, and she had to make the hearts! That was bad. Really bad.

Katie looked at the clock. It was 5:15 already and the mailman was coming at 6:00! That didn't leave much time.

She jumped up and raced into the kitchen. She had spotted some of the big candy hearts there on a shelf. Katie grabbed three of them and laid them out on Cinnamon's work area. She picked up the candy chisel from the counter. She'd seen Cinnamon make the hearts just the other day, when she and Jeremy were at the shop. Chiseling messages hadn't looked so hard then.

The messages! Oh, no! Katie had torn them up. She had no idea what she was supposed to write!

Quickly, she zoomed back into the front of the shop and picked up all the little scraps of paper. Uh-oh. She'd *really* torn them up. It was impossible to make out what words the girls had written.

But Katie was going to have to try. "It's just like a puzzle," she told herself. "All I have to do is put the pieces together."

Eventually, Katie actually managed to put together some messages. But the sentences didn't make a whole lot of sense. At least not to her.

She looked up at the clock. Yikes! There was no more time to figure things out. She'd have to work with what she had.

All she could do was start writing and hope for the best.

Chapter 9

Katie was just putting the last address label on the candy boxes when the mail carrier arrived. He knocked on the door, and Katie let him into the shop.

"Hi, Cinnamon," he greeted her. "Closing early today?"

"I, um, I had to make a lot of candy, so I shut the shop," Katie answered quickly.

"You have any packages for me?"

Katie nodded. "Just these three boxes. They're all going to Cherrydale Elementary School."

"The elementary school!" the mailman exclaimed. "Boy, oh, boy. Don't kids just send those little paper cards anymore?"

Katie shrugged. "Some do. These girls didn't think that was enough, I guess."

"Kids today," the mail carrier sighed.

"I know," Katie agreed, sounding very much like a grown-up.

"This is a busy time of year for both of us." He patted his mailbag and smiled. "Love is definitely in the air."

Katie rolled her eyes. "Yes, it is," she replied.

"Well, see ya tomorrow," he said as he took the boxes and left the shop.

Katie locked the door behind him and took a deep breath. She was glad she'd managed to get the hearts finished in time. Now all she had to do was clean up the mess she'd made in the kitchen. Katie was not a very neat candy maker. There was sugar everywhere!

But as soon as she walked into the kitchen, Katie felt a slight draft on the back of her neck. She didn't have to look to see if there was a breeze anywhere else in the shop. She knew there wouldn't be.

The magic wind was back.

And *that* wind only blew around Katie.

The magic wind picked up speed, spinning wildly around her like a full-blown tornado. Katie gripped onto the kitchen counter and shut her eyes tight.

And then the wind stopped. Just like that.

Katie opened her eyes slowly and looked around. She was still in the shop's kitchen. But she wasn't alone anymore. Cinnamon was there, too. She looked very confused.

"What happened here?" Cinnamon asked Katie. "This place is a mess."

"I think you were in a hurry to get those candy hearts finished," Katie told her.

"Candy hearts?"

Katie nodded. "You know the ones that Jessica, Mandy, and Becky ordered?"

"Oh, yeah," Cinnamon said. "I have to make those. Or did I already do that? I'm not

sure. It's all kind of foggy."

"You made them, and you gave them to the mailman," Katie assured her.

Cinnamon shook her head and sat down on a stool. "I think I need to get a breath of fresh air," she said. "I'm going to take a walk."

"Okay," Katie said quickly.

"Do you want me to help clean up?" Katie asked.

"No. I'll straighten the kitchen when I get back. After all, *I* made the mess."

Katie frowned. Not exactly. But she couldn't explain that to Cinnamon. "Okay, bye!" she shouted as she darted out of the store as fast as she could.

Chapter 10

Katie groaned as her alarm clock went off on Friday morning. She was not looking forward to this day. Today, class 4A was celebrating Valentine's Day. And Katie hated Valentine's Day.

"Happy Valentine's Day, sleepyhead," Katie's mom called cheerfully as she walked into Katie's room.

"Grr . . ." Katie pulled the covers over her head.

"I got you an early Valentine's Day gift," her mother said, peeling back the covers and handing Katie a small package.

Katie unwrapped the gift and sighed.

Inside was a package of new tights—white ones with tiny black hearts on them.

"I thought you could wear them to your class party today," Mrs. Carew suggested.

Katie didn't want to disappoint her mother. "Thanks, Mom," she said, forcing a smile.

× × ×

Katie's new tights fit right in with her classroom. On Friday, class 4A was the Valentine's Day capital of the world! Mr. Guthrie had made a giant mobile with all the cards he'd received from his students. It was hanging from the ceiling. Cardboard cupids flew joyously over the blackboard, and red construction paper hearts were plastered to the side of Slinky's glass tank. Katie thought the whole room looked horrible!

And of course, all the kids had decorated their beanbag chairs with the cards they'd given one another. *All the kids except Katie, that is.* Her beanbag wasn't decorated at all.

Katie spent most of the morning watching

the door to her classroom. The candy hearts would be delivered sometime today. She didn't know when. But she did know that once they were, there would be big trouble.

The boys were already sick of all the girls looking at them and giggling. When they got those candy hearts, they were going to go *crazy*!

But there weren't any special deliveries that morning. By lunchtime, Katie began to relax. Maybe the hearts weren't coming after all. Maybe Katie had gotten something wrong on the address labels. Or maybe the school didn't let kids get mail during the school day, or . . .

No such luck!

As soon as the fourth grade entered the lunchroom, Mrs. Davidson, the school secretary, walked in. She was carrying three big boxes.

"I have special packages," she announced. "Will Jeremy Fox, Andrew Epstein, and Kevin Camilleri come get their mail?"

Katie gulped. This was the moment Katie had been dreading.

Jeremy was the first boy to open his box. "Oh, no, it's a heart," he groaned.

Becky ran over to him. "It says just how I feel."

"Ooooh," the boys teased.

Jeremy read the message on the candy.

"Huh?" Jeremy asked.

"She thinks she can crush you," Kadeem laughed. "That's just wrong, dude."

Katie looked over at Jeremy. He looked furious!

Becky looked down at the heart. "That's not the message I wrote," she insisted. She sounded like she was going to cry.

Andrew was the next to open his box. "Who is this from?" he asked.

"Mandy," Suzanne and Jessica shouted out.

Mandy blushed. Andrew blushed harder as he opened the box.

"Love your what?" Andrew asked her.

Mandy looked at the heart curiously. "That's not right. Cinnamon was *supposed* to write 'Won't You *Be* Mine?' "

"Well, I won't," Andrew told her.

Now it was Kevin's turn.

"Oh, look, it's *another* lover boy!" George squealed, making his voice go up really high.

"Ooh, Kev's got a girlfriend," Manny added.

"Why me?" Kevin moaned. As he opened his box, Kevin looked like he was going to be sick. But when he read the heart, a smile returned to his face.

"I don't have a secret admirer after all," he said as he held up the candy heart. "This isn't for me!"

Kevin turned proudly to the guys. "See, it's for some people named Val and Tim."

"It's not supposed to say that!" Jessica

announced suddenly. "It was supposed to say 'Love, Your Secret Valentine'!"

Oops! Now everyone knew Jessica was Kevin's secret admirer.

"Jessica and Kevin sitting in a tree," George began to sing. "K-I-S-S-I-N-G."

That made Kevin plenty mad. "Stop it, George. Or I'll tell everyone you still sleep with a teddy bear."

That sure made Kadeem laugh. "A teddy bear! What a baby!" he exclaimed.

Now *George* was mad. "You swore you'd never tell," he shouted at Kevin.

"*I'll* tell you something. I'm never going back to that candy store!" Becky announced.

"Me, neither," Mandy agreed.

"I'll never forgive Cinnamon for this," Jessica added.

Katie frowned. *This was so not good*.

Chapter 11

After school, Katie went to the mall with her mother. Mrs. Carew had to stop by the Book Nook to wait for an order of books that was due to arrive.

As they passed by Cinnamon's Candy Shop, Katie got very sad. Usually, the store would be filled with kids buying penny candy. But today there were only adults in there—buying last-minute gifts, Katie guessed.

"Katie!" Cinnamon came running out of the store as Katie and her mom walked by.

"Oh, hi," Katie said quietly.

"Weren't you going to visit me today?" asked Cinnamon.

Katie had been too ashamed of what she had done to visit Cinnamon. "Well, I, uh . . ." she began.

"You know, it's the strangest thing," Cinnamon told Katie and her mother. "None of the fourth-graders have come to the store today. Usually they're here by now."

"That *is* strange," Mrs. Carew agreed. "Your store has become quite a hangout."

"I know. But today, they all just walked by. Some of the girls even looked angry with me."

Now Katie felt *really* bad. "You don't think you'll go out of business, do you?" she asked nervously.

Cinnamon smiled kindly. "No, sweetie. I actually make most of my money from adults who buy chocolate gift boxes. I just *like* having the kids around. That's why I opened a candy store. Kids always come when there's candy around." She paused for a moment. "At least they did until now."

"Do you have any idea what might have

changed?" Mrs. Carew asked.

Cinnamon shook her head. "That's the strange thing."

Katie knew what was wrong. She also knew it was all her fault.

Just then, Katie got one of her great ideas. "You should have a party!" she blurted out.

"A party?" Cinnamon asked.

Katie nodded. "A great big Valentine's Day party. With balloons and music. I'll bet the kids would come to that. I could call all the fourth-graders and invite them."

Cinnamon thought for a moment. "I could give out little bags of candy hearts as favors."

Katie flinched. "I think the kids have had enough of those," she said quickly. "Maybe you could just give out regular candies."

Cinnamon shrugged. "Okay. I'll do it. I hope this brings the kids back to the store."

So do I, Katie thought to herself.

× × ×

"But you *have* to come, Suzanne," Katie begged her best friend. The girls were talking to one another on the phone later that evening. "If you don't, nobody will."

"Well, I *do* set the trends in our grade," Suzanne agreed.

Katie sighed. Suzanne was such a show-off. But she wasn't wrong. Most of the girls *did* copy whatever Suzanne did.

"Still, Cinnamon really messed things up," Suzanne continued.

"Not for you," Katie told her. "Your heart came to your house Wednesday night. It said exactly what it was supposed to."

"I guess," Suzanne agreed. "But . . ."

"Cinnamon probably only made the mistakes since she was rushing. You guys did have a last-minute order, after all. Cinnamon is a really nice person," Katie said. "She keeps secrets really well."

"What's that supposed to mean?" Suzanne asked.

"She didn't tell anyone about your secret admirer," Katie told her.

"She said she couldn't."

"I know," Katie agreed. "But *I* can tell if I want to."

"Tell what?" Suzanne sounded nervous.

"Who your secret admirer is. I figured it out. But I kept your secret. And so did Cinnamon. You owe us."

Suzanne was quiet for a minute. Katie crossed her fingers. She would never really tell Suzanne's secret, but this was the only plan she had. Katie hoped it would work!

"All right," Suzanne agreed. "I'll come."

Katie was relieved. "And you'll get some of the other girls to come, too?"

"I'll try," Suzanne said slowly.

Katie smiled as she hung up the phone. That took care of the girls. Now she had to deal with the boys.

Quickly, she dialed Jeremy's phone number. When he answered the phone, she told him all about the party.

"I'm not going anywhere near there," he told Katie. "I'm staying as far from Becky as I can."

"I don't think that's too smart," Katie replied.

"Why?"

"Well, look what happened the last time Becky went to Cinnamon's. She got you a heart. At least if you're there, you can make sure she doesn't do anything like that again."

Jeremy was quiet for a moment. Finally, he said, "I guess you're right."

"I know I am," Katie assured him. "We'll go to the party right after our cooking club meeting. It'll be fun, I promise."

Chapter 12

Katie spent the whole evening calling her friends. Her phone calls really worked. Almost everyone in the fourth grade agreed to come to Cinnamon's Valentine's Day party.

The next day, the kids arrived at Cinnamon's Candy Shop. But they didn't look like they were in the mood to party. Instead, they all looked angry. The girls still hadn't forgiven Cinnamon for what was written on their hearts. And the boys hadn't forgiven the girls for sending the hearts in the first place.

Cinnamon wasn't about to let the kids have a bad time. She just kept smiling and handing out candy. Her smiles—and her sweets—were too much to ignore.

"Wow! Free candy!" Jeremy exclaimed. "Awesome."

"Can I have some more jelly beans?" George asked Cinnamon.

"Sure," Cinnamon replied. She handed him a bag of red and white ones. "Eat up."

"Woohoo!" George exclaimed.

"This is my favorite song," Suzanne said as a Bayside Boys song came on the radio. She started to dance.

So did Jessica. She *always* did whatever Suzanne was doing.

"Admit it. Cinnamon throws a great party," Katie said, dancing over to the girls.

"Yeah, well, she owed it to us after the mess she made," Jessica told Katie.

"But I think we can find it in our *hearts* to forgive her," Suzanne said.

Jessica laughed. "I guess so."

Before long, it seemed as though everyone had put the candy heart mess behind them. They just wanted to have a good time.

But no one was having as good a time as Cinnamon. Seeing her smiling again almost made Katie forget just how much she hated Valentine's Day.

"Come in the back room with me," Cinnamon said as she walked over to put her arm around Katie. "I have a special surprise."

"For me?"

Cinnamon nodded. "I think you'll like it."

Katie followed Cinnamon back into the kitchen.

"Here you go." Cinnamon handed Katie a big cardboard box.

Katie smiled as she quickly whipped the top off of the box. Inside was a candy heart that read:

"Valentine's Day is a nice time to thank your friends for how happy they make you," Cinnamon explained.

Katie smiled. "I never thought of it that way," she admitted. "I figured it was just about love and crushes and mushy stuff."

Cinnamon shook her head. "It doesn't have

to be." Cinnamon peeked out into the front of the shop. The kids were laughing, talking, and snacking on candy. "See, no one's acting mushy out there."

"Do you think this whole *crush* thing is over?" Katie asked hopefully.

"For now," Cinnamon told her.

That was going to have to be good enough. "In that case, I have to leave for a few minutes," Katie said suddenly.

"Leave? Why?"

"I have to get to the pet shop. I didn't get Pepper a valentine this year. And he's my very best friend. Maybe they have a heart-shaped liver treat for him."

Cinnamon made a face. "*Liver?* Yuck. I'm glad I make treats for *people*."

Katie laughed.

"Happy Valentine's Day," Cinnamon said as Katie turned to leave.

"Happy Valentine's Day," Katie answered. And she really meant it.

A Card Idea from Katie Kazoo to You!

Are you puzzled about what kind of Valentine's Day card to send to *your* friends? This jigsaw-puzzle card is a great way to give a piece of your heart.

You will need:

A sheet of thick cardboard

A photo of you and your friend together

Markers

Glue

Scissors

An envelope

Here's what you do:

1. Glue the photograph of you and your friend onto the piece of cardboard.

2. Use the markers to decorate the rest of the cardboard. Don't forget to write your name!

3. Cut the cardboard into jigsaw puzzle pieces. Make them all different shapes and sizes.

4. Place the puzzle pieces into an envelope and give them to your friend. Your pal is sure to have a fun time putting the card together!